Enid Blyton's

MAGICAL TALES

The Dancing Doll
and other stories

This is a Parragon Book

© Parragon 1997

13-17 Avonbridge Trading Estate,
Atlantic Road, Avonmouth, Bristol
Produced by The Templar Company plc,
Pippbrook Mill, London Road, Dorking,
Surrey RH4 1JE

Text copyright © Enid Blyton Ltd 1926-29

These stories were first published in Sunny Stories,
Teacher's Treasury, Two Years in the Infant School,
Read to Us, New Friends and Old and
The Daily Mail Annual.

Enid Blyton's signature mark is a registered
trademark of Enid Blyton Limited.

Edited by Caroline Repchuk and Dugald Steer

Designed by Mark Kingsley-Monks

Printed and bound in Italy

ISBN 0 7525 1706 6 (Hardback)
ISBN 0 7525 2324 4 (Paperback)

Enid Blyton's

MAGICAL TALES

The Dancing Doll

and other stories

PARRAGON

Contents

The
Dancing Doll

THERE was once a little dancing doll who lived on the windowsill of Mary's playroom. She was the prettiest little thing, with a key in her back. When she was wound up she would put out her arms this way and that, and dance round and round on her small feet.

As she lived on the windowsill she had no friends among the toys, who all lived together in the playroom cupboard. But she had one very good friend – and that was the blackbird who had a nest in the apple tree outside. He had a wife, and they had brought up three fine youngsters in their cosy nest. The dancing doll could see them from the windowsill, and loved to watch them.

The blackbird was very fond of the dancing doll, because she had helped him to win his wife that spring. There had been another blackbird in the garden, and both had wanted to marry the dark brown hen bird. She could not make up her mind – and first she looked at one and then she looked at the other! Which one should she marry?

The blackbird who was friendly with the dancing doll had gone to the apple tree, and had moped miserably. The doll had seen

him, and called to him to know
what was the matter. When she
heard his tale, she smiled at him.

"I will make you very beautiful
and shiny," she said. "Then the
hen will think you are lovely, and
will marry you – and you can
build your nest in this tree so
that I may watch you, for I am
sometimes lonely sitting on my
window-sill here, away from all
the other toys."

The blackbird hopped onto the
sill. The doll lifted up the
window seat, and got out from
the cupboard underneath a
duster and a tin of polish which
Mummy kept there. She put

some polish on the duster, and then rubbed the blackbird's beak hard. Soon it began to shine and gleam a bright orange-gold, beautiful to see!

Then the doll lifted up the lid again and took out some of the black shoe polish that Daddy used for cleaning Mary's shoes. She put some on the duster, and began to polish the blackbird's black coat.

You should have seen it when she had finished! It was as bright as a mirror! Off he flew in delight, and when the hen saw his beautiful glossy coat, and heard the glad song he sang from his gleaming golden beak, she fell in love with him at once, and married him.

So you can guess that the little doll was great friends with the blackbird.

"Some day I will do you a good turn too," promised the blackbird. And that day came, as you will hear.

One morning the blackbird found the dancing doll in tears on the window-sill. "What is the matter?" he asked.

"A horrid great bird came this morning and took away my nice shining key," sobbed the doll. "Now I cannot be wound up, so I shall never dance again. I am so very unhappy."

"What sort of bird was it?" asked the blackbird.

"It was a great big bird, all black, except that he had a grey patch at the back of his neck," said the doll. "Oh, blackbird, do you think you can help me?"

"I'll try," said the blackbird. "That bird was a jackdaw. Jackdaws love shiny things, and often steal them and hide them. He may have put your key in his nest for his young ones to play with. I will go and see."

He flew off. He knew where the jackdaw had his nest – high

up in the church tower. He flew up and up and at last came to the tower. He perched on the edge of the tower and looked inside it. Sure enough, there was the jackdaw's nest. He had almost filled up the tower with sticks, and in the middle of them he had built his big nest!

"Good morning," said the blackbird. "Come up here and talk to me."

The jackdaw flew off his nest and perched beside the blackbird, always ready for a chat. The blackbird saw the gleam of something shiny in the nest, and he knew that the doll's key was there!

"How are your young ones getting on?" asked the blackbird.

"Very well," said the jackdaw, "but they are always so hungry that I find it quite difficult to feed them."

"I know where there are some lovely, fat, juicy caterpillars," said the blackbird.

"Oh, do tell me," begged the jackdaw eagerly.

"What will you give me if I do?" asked the blackbird.

"I have nothing to give you," said the jackdaw. "Well – I only have a little shining thing, of no use to anyone."

"I will have that, I think," said the blackbird. So the jackdaw hopped down to his nest, and picked up the key in his beak. He gave it to the blackbird.

"The caterpillars are in the nettles at the end of the turnip field," said the blackbird, and flew off at once with the key, afraid that the jackdaw might change his mind at any moment!

He flew down to the window-sill, and the doll gave a scream of delight when she saw her key in his bright beak.

"Oh, you are a darling!" she said. "You really are!"

"I know where there is a piece

of string," said the clever blackbird. "I will get it – and then you can tie the key to yourself, Dancing Doll – so that if the jackdaw comes again, he will not be able to take it away!"

He wound up the doll – and she danced merrily for him. Then off he flew to get the string. And now the key is tied tightly to the doll, so that the jackdaw will not be able to get it any more.

"It is nice to have a friend!" said the doll, hugging the blackbird. And, do you know, she was quite right!

The Toys and the Goblins

ONCE upon a time, when the toys in the playroom were quietly playing hide-and-seek in the middle of the night, there came a small tap-tap-tapping at the window.

"What's that?" whispered the brown teddy bear in a fright.

"Please, oh, please let us in!" cried a small voice. "We are the little blue fairies who live at the bottom of the garden. We have been chased by the big red goblin, and he will soon be after us again!"

Quickly the teddy bear and the sailor doll opened the window, and in climbed a troop of tiny blue fairies, all as pale as moonlight with fright.

"Goodness!" cried the sailor doll in astonishment. "Whatever can have happened to your lovely wings?"

"Oh isn't it perfectly dreadful!" wept the first fairy. "The red goblin came whilst we were all sleeping the other night and cut all of our wings off!" She turned around and showed her clipped wings to the toys. "That goblin wants us all to be his servants, you know, for he has a big house up on the hillside, and he wants us to go and live there and keep it clean for him."

"But we have always said no,"
said another very small fairy.
"He is a nasty creature. He is
terribly unkind, and so none of
us fairies will have anything to
do with him at all. We thought
we would fly far away to our
aunt, who lives up in the clouds,
but before we could do that the
horrible goblin came and cut our
wings off."

"Yes," said the first fairy,
wiping away her tears, "and if a
big green frog hadn't happened
to hop up and help us, then the
goblin would have taken us all
that very minute – but we
managed to escape, by running

away as fast as we could."

"Did he come after you again?" asked the sailor doll, looking very fierce.

"Oh, yes, he came again the very next night," said the tiny fairy. "We had hidden in the pansy bed but an unkind snail told him where we were and so he managed to hunt us out again. Then we hid ourselves under a mossy stone but he managed to find us there as well – and tonight, just as we were sleeping in the hollow oak tree, we heard him coming again – so we thought we would come to you for shelter."

"I'm very glad you did," said the big teddy bear, kindly. "You shall stay here with us as long as you like. There is plenty of room for you all in the toy cupboard. If that nasty old goblin comes looking for you we'll soon frighten him off!"

"He said he would go and get twelve more goblins to help him come and fetch us," said the fairy. "Do you think you could manage to fight so many?"

The toys looked grave. The sailor doll shook his head.

"No," he said. "I don't think we could possibly fight so many goblins. You see we are only toys, and we're not very strong. But won't your wings grow back again, fairies?"

"Oh, yes," said the little creatures, nodding their golden heads. "But not for a week or two. If only we could stay here in safety for about a fortnight, our wings would grow properly again and we could spread them out and fly off to our aunt quite easily. Then the goblin couldn't possibly come and get us."

"Well, you must stay with us, then," said the bear. "We will keep a good look-out for the goblin, and if he does come with his friends we will save you

somehow. We have a friend in
the garden, a red-breasted robin.
We will ask him to watch and see
what the wicked goblin is doing,
and if he comes to tell us that the
goblins are all coming here to get
you, we will hide you away safely
somewhere."

So the blue fairies cheered up
and were soon very happy. The
toy train gave them a fine ride all
round the playroom, and the big
bus ran them to and fro on the
rug till his clockwork nearly
broke down!

Some of the fairies squeezed
into the brick box and the others
found room in the doll's cot,

when they were sleepy at cock-crow. The toys went back to their cupboard, and soon there was nothing to be seen or heard in the quiet playroom.

When the sun rose the robin came peeping in at the window. The sailor doll saw him and beckoned to him. The little bird flew into the room. Very soon the toys had told him all about the goblins and he promised to keep an eye on them and to tell the toys at once, if he heard that they were coming to the playroom. Off he flew, and the fairies heard him trilling a cheery little song in the tree outside.

Day after day went by and there was no sign of the red goblin. The robin came to see the toys each day and told them that everything was safe.

"The goblin is in his house on the hill," he sang. "He has not been to see any of the other goblins. Perhaps he has decided not to bother the blue fairies any more!"

The fairies were delighted. It was very pleasant living in the playroom. When Ann, the girl whose playroom it was, came to play with the toys, the fairies often peeped out to watch. Ann had no idea at all that they were staying there, of course – but wouldn't she have been excited if she had seen them!

Each night the sailor doll turned the fairies round and looked at their clipped wings.

"Yes," he would say, his head on one side, "Yes, your wings are certainly growing fast again! They are bigger than last night. In a few days you all will be able to fly away safely to your aunt's house up in the clouds, and you won't have to worry about the goblin again!"

In a little while both toys and fairies began to forget the red goblin, for the robin never had

any news of him. They felt quite
sure that he had given up all
hope of catching the fairies, and
nobody worried any more.

So it was a dreadful shock to
hear the robin singing in alarm
one morning at sunrise. His voice
was loud and he tapped at the
window-pane.

"The goblin is coming tonight,
tonight!" he sang. "He has
twelve friends coming to help
him! Yes, he has, he has! He sent
them all a letter, and now they
have promised to help him this
very evening. What will you do,
what will you do? Are the fairies'
wings grown yet?"

"No, no!" cried the sailor doll in fright, and he pushed up the window to let in the robin. "They are too small for the fairies to fly with yet, they are only half the size they should be. It takes two weeks for wings to grow again. Oh my, oh my, whatever are we to do?"

The fairies began to cry, for they felt very frightened. "Oh, please, do think of some plan to help us!" they begged the toys. "You are so clever, so wise!"

Just then the toys heard a door opening downstairs and they knew it was Mummy, who was up and ready to air the rooms and

make the breakfast. So they
scurried back to the toy
cupboard with the fairies, feeling
frightened and worried.
Whatever were they going to do?
The goblins would be sure to
come that very night – and how
were they going to save the poor
little fairies? If only, only, only
they could get them away to
their aunt who lived up in the
clouds! Then they would be quite
safe from the goblin and his
twelve friends.

All that day the toys thought
and thought. The sailor doll
frowned – the teddy bear
groaned. What could they do?

Ann played with them as usual, but they couldn't even feel happy when they were with her. At last she put them down and opened a box she had found at the back of the cupboard.

Inside it there was a wooden pipe, some soap flakes and a small bowl – it was a bubble-blowing set.

"This will be fun!" said Ann. "I'll blow some bubbles for a change!" So she mixed the soap flakes in some water, dipped her pipe in the bowl and began to blow some beautiful big bubbles, which floated away through the open window and into the sunshine. The toys watched in wonder – it really was a most beautiful sight.

And then the sailor doll had a marvellous idea – so marvellous that he could hardly wait for the night to come to tell the others. But at last the playroom was in darkness except for the moonlight that streamed in through the window, and the sailor doll hurriedly called the toys and fairies round him.

"I know how to save the fairies from the goblins!" he cried. "Did you see Ann blowing those lovely bubbles? Well, why don't we blow some too, and each of

the tiny fairies can slip inside a
bubble and be blown out of the
window and right up to the
clouds! Then they will all be
quite safe!"

"What a wonderful idea!" cried
everyone, and the fairies shouted
in delight. So the sailor doll went
to the cupboard and got out the
bubble box. The clown climbed
up to the wash-basin, turned on
the tap, and put some hot water
into the bubble bowl. Then the
sailor doll dipped the wooden
pipe into the bowl and stirred up
the flakes there till there was a
lovely, soapy lather.

Just at that moment the robin

tapped on the window. "The goblins are coming, the goblins are coming!" he trilled. "I kept awake tonight to see – and I have just spied them creeping up the garden in a big crowd."

The blue fairies began to cry. The teddy bear comforted them and told the sailor doll to hurry up as much as he possible could. The sailor doll at once began to blow bubbles. You should have seen them! He blew beautiful big ones, all shining and glittering, and as he blew each one one of the tiny little fairies would slip inside and waited for the bubble to get bigger.

Then the teddy bear blew it off the pipe and all the toys puffed and puffed till the bubble floated out of the window and up into the sky.

"Once we are at our aunts we shall be safe!" cried the fairies. "Goodbye, dear toys! Goodbye, all of you, and thank you for all your kindness. We'll come and see you again when our wings have grown."

Just then there came some loud shouts and growls and up on to the window-sill swarmed a crowd of red goblins, with wicked, shining eyes and long, pointed ears. They shook their fists at the

toys and cried: "Where are all
those fairies? Where have you
hidden them? Tell us at once, or
it will be the worse for you!"

Only two small blue fairies
were left by now. All the others
had safely floated off in the
bubbles. The toys quickly stood
in front of the two fairies, and
the sailor doll went on blowing
bubbles quite calmly.

The goblins climbed into the
playroom and ran to the toy
cupboard to hunt for the fairies.
The sailor doll blew a fine
bubble and one of the two fairies
slipped inside it. Off she went,
floating through the window and

up into the air. Then the sailor
doll blew another bubble and the
last fairy squeezed into it. He
blew it bigger, and the bear
puffed it off the bowl of the pipe.
It rose towards the window and
all the toys blew hard. It floated
out and up into the air – and just
at that very moment the goblins
saw the fairy inside it!

How they shouted! How they
yelled! How they shook their
fists! But it wasn't a bit of good –
the little blue fairies were all
gone, every single one. They had
all safely escaped!

All the noise woke up Ann,
who was asleep in her bedroom

nearby. She sat up in bed and listened. There certainly was a noise! The goblins were attacking the toys, who were trying to fight back, but dear me, the goblins were far too fierce for them!

Just as the goblins were about to take the frightened toys prisoner, Ann came pattering to the door. At once the goblins fled out of the window, and the toys rushed back to the toy cupboard. Ann found no one about – but to her very great surprise, there, in the middle of the floor was her bubble set, with the wooden pipe still in the soapy water!

She was astonished! "Now who in the world has been playing with that?" she wondered. "How strange! I should love to know."

But nobody ever told her – though if she had listened very carefully to the robin's song that winter she might have heard the whole story. Anyway, that's how I got to know all about it!

The Dog, the Cat and the Duck

ONCE upon a time there lived a little girl called Anna who was taken prisoner by a witch. She lived in the witch's cottage, and did all the work – dusting, sweeping, cooking and mending. Often she tried to run away, but there was a high hedge all round the little garden, and search as she might, Anna could never find the way out – only the witch knew that.

"Oh dear, oh dear!" Anna would sigh. "I suppose I must stay here all my life, working for that horrid old witch!"

Now, with the witch lived a dog, a cat and a duck. The dog

used to lie out in the garden all night, guarding the cottage. The cat used to help the old witch with her spells, by standing with her for hours inside a chalk circle which the witch drew on the cottage floor – and the duck used to quack a magic song while the spell was going on.

At first the animals took no notice of Anna. They ate the food that she gave them, growled, spat and quacked at each other, and made sure they kept in their own corners.

"Don't you ever speak to them," the witch warned Anna. "They are quarrelsome, ill-natured creatures. The cat would scratch, the dog would bite, and the duck would peck if you ever tried to make friends with them."

So Anna left them well alone, until one morning, after a very cold, snowy night, the poor dog crept in shivering from his night watch. He went and lay down by the fire, and Anna felt very sorry for him.

Suddenly she had an idea. She waited until the witch had gone out, then she quickly got her little work basket.

She found some red flannel, and began to sew quickly. From

time to time she looked at the shivering dog, who lay and growled at the cat whenever she wanted to share the fire.

Anna smiled as she sewed – for she was making a red flannel coat for the dog!

"It will keep him lovely and warm at night!" she thought. "But, dear me! I don't know how ever I shall get him to let me put it on him! I expect he'll try to bite me!"

She sewed on the buttons, and at last it was finished. She picked it up and looked at the dog.

"See!" she said gently. "Here is a nice coat to keep you warm at night. Let me try it on you!"

The dog growled.

"Come!" said Anna, showing him the coat. "Let me see if it will fit you!"

The dog stopped growling and looked at her. Rather afraid, Anna went over to him and patted his head. He stared at her in surprise. He had never been patted in his life before, and he liked it very, very much. To Anna's immense surprise, he started to speak!

"Do that again!" he said in an odd, husky voice.

She patted him again, and he put his great head on her knee.

Quickly she slipped the red coat round him and buttoned it. It fitted him perfectly!

The dog twisted and turned himself about to look at it. It felt warm and comfortable. Then he looked at Anna.

"No one has ever been kind to me before," he said. "Thank you. Now I shall be warm at night. But do not let the witch see it! I will come to your room morning and night, for you to put the coat on or take it off. Quick! Here comes the witch. Hide it!"

Anna took the coat off quickly, and put it at the bottom of her basket. Then she began mending

a hole in her stocking, and when
the witch came in she didn't
notice anything.

Every night the dog came to
have his coat put on, and every
morning early he slipped through
the window of Anna's room to
have it taken off. Anna felt
happier than she had been, for
she knew the dog liked her. She
wondered if she could do
anything for the cat.

"She must get terribly cold feet
standing on that stone floor for
so long, when the witch makes
magic!" she thought. "Shall I
knit her some little black socks?
The witch would never notice

them on the cat's black paws!"

She set to work and knitted four funny little black socks. When she had finished them, she took them to the big black cat.

"See," said Anna kindly. "Here are some little socks for you to wear when you are standing on the cold floor while the witch makes magic!"

Now the cat had watched Anna being kind to the dog, and had wished she would be kind to her as well. So she purred gratefully, instead of scratching, and let Anna slip on the funny little socks. They fitted perfectly!

"Thank you!" said the cat.

"You are the first person who has been kind to me! These socks will keep my feet nice and warm. Hide them in your room, and when I have to help the witch, I will run through and ask you to put them on. She will never see them, for they are just as black as my fur!"

So Anna had another friend, and she smiled to see the cat standing solemnly by the witch every day with a little black sock on each paw!

One day the duck, who had been standing for two hours quacking a magic song for the witch, came to the little girl, and looked at her, and to Anna's great surprise, the bird spoke!

"You have been kind to the dog, and good to the cat," said the duck in a hoarse voice, "will you be kind to me too?"

"Why, certainly," said Anna, very pleased indeed. "What can I do for you?"

"All that quacking makes my throat very sore," said the duck. "Make me a scarf that I can wear round my neck when the witch isn't here."

"Of course I will," said Anna, and set to work at once. She knitted a long, blue woollen scarf, and the duck liked it very much indeed.

So Anna had three friends, and one day she wondered if they could help her to escape.

That evening, when the witch was out riding her broomstick, Anna sat down by the fire with the dog, the cat and the duck.

"Listen," she said. "I want to escape from here. Do you know the way out?"

"I don't," said the dog.

"I don't," said the cat.

"And I don't," said the duck.

Anna sighed.

"But I've got an idea!" said the dog.

"So have I," said the cat.

"And so have I," said the duck.

"What?" asked Anna.

"Take the witch's broomstick when she's asleep!" said all three together.

"It will fly over the tall hedge," said the dog.

"And right up into the sky," said the cat.

"And away to your home," said the duck.

So that night Anna stole into the kitchen and took the broomstick from its corner. She opened the door, and slipped out with the cat, who was wearing her socks, and the duck, who was wearing her scarf. In the garden was the dog, waiting for her patiently with his red coat on.

"Sit on the broomstick and say:
'Ringa-maree,
Listen to me,
Ringa-maray,
Take me away!'"
said the dog.

Anna sat down on the broomstick and looked at her three friends.

"I don't like leaving you," she said sadly.

"I'll come with you," said the dog, and jumped on to the broomstick.

"And so will I," said the cat, and sat down on the broom.

"And so will I," said the duck, and perched right on the very end of the broomstick.

"Ringa-maree,
Listen to me,
Ringa-maray,
Take me away!"
said Anna.

And whizz-whizz-whizz! The broomstick rose in the air and flew right over the tall hedge, taking Anna, the dog, the cat and the duck with it.

All that night they flew, under the moon and the stars, and when the dawn came, the dog gave a growl, the cat a mew and the duck a quack!

"Whatever's the matter?" asked Anna.

"That horrible witch is after us!" said the dog.

Sure enough, far away in the distance was a little black speck running on the ground.

"Take my coat off," begged the dog. Anna did so, and the dog took it and flung it down to the ground far below.

Immediately it grew bigger and bigger, until it lay like a stretch of rough country just in front of the witch. The buttons became big rocks, and the four friends watched the witch stop in dismay.

"That will stop her!" chuckled

the dog. "It's a good thing you made me a coat, Anna!"

On they flew, on and on and on. After a short time the three animals all looked downwards once again.

"Quack!" said the duck. "There she is!"

Anna saw the witch below them. She had climbed over the big rocks and left the stretch of rough country behind. Now she was hurrying after them again to catch them, ready to turn them into beetles, spiders and toads as soon as she came near enough.

"Oh dear!" said Anna. "What shall we do?"

"Just wait a minute!" said the cat, and pulled off one of her little black socks. She threw it down in the witch's path. Directly it touched the ground, it swelled and swelled and became a great rocky hill up which the witch had to climb.

After a little while the cat drew off another sock and dropped that down too. It swelled into a bigger hill than the first one.

Then the cat flung down her two other socks, and Anna watched them rise up into enormous hills to stop the witch and make her lose her way.

"That will stop her!" chuckled

the cat. "It's a good thing you made me those socks, Anna!"

Anna watched the witch running down the first hill. She came to the second hill, and began slowly climbing up that.

"I really think we're safe now!" said Anna. "We shall be quite out of sight soon. Hurry up broomstick!"

On they went again, till suddenly Anna gave a cry of delight – for there below her lay her home, and there was her mother hanging clothes up on the line.

Down went the broomstick to the ground – but just as it

reached the grass, the duck quacked loudly in fright. And there was the old witch hurrying towards them, a horrid smile on her ugly face.

"Untie my scarf and throw it at her," begged the duck.

Anna quickly untied it and flung it at the witch. Immediately it turned into a river of blue, and Splash! the witch fell straight into it and was drowned.

So that was the end of her. As for Anna, she ran to her mother and hugged her and hugged her, and told her all that had happened, till her mother could hardly believe her ears.

"And here are my three friends," said Anna at last, and showed her mother the dog, the cat, and the duck.

"They must live with us!" said Anna's mother – and they did. And as the dog guarded them well, and the cat taught them magic spells, and the duck laid them silver eggs every day, you can guess they soon got rich and lived happily ever after.

The
Christmas
Party

DONALD was a lonely boy, for he had no brothers or sisters, and instead of going to school his mother taught him his lessons. So he had no friends and no one to play with. And will you believe it, he had never been asked to a party in his life!

At Christmas time he used to peep into other people's windows and see the children dancing round the Christmas tree and pulling crackers. He did so long to join them, but no one ever asked him.

One day, just after Christmas, Donald dressed himself up in the Red Indian suit that his mother had given him for Christmas. He looked very fine in the leather tunic, fringed trousers and enormous feathered head-dress. Just as he had finished dressing he looked out of the window and saw that there was a party next door. It was a fancy dress party too! All the children that arrived were dressed up as fairies, clowns, milk-maids or soldiers.

"I'll go and watch them arriving," thought Donald. "That will be fun." So he slipped out of his front door and watched the children arrive. When they had all come he saw them playing nuts and may in the front room.

So he went over to their front gate and watched.

Presently the door opened and a lady ran down to the gate. She took Donald's hand and pulled him to the door. "Here's a late little boy!" she called. "He's too shy to come in. Look at his beautiful fancy dress!"

Donald tried to explain that he hadn't been asked to the party, but nobody listened to him. Soon he found himself playing musical chairs and general post, and then, dear me, he was sitting down to a most glorious tea! After that there was a conjuror who made a rabbit come out of

Donald's tunic and two pennies out of his ears! Then there was a wonderful Christmas tree and Donald was given a fine trumpet and a box of chocolates.

All the other children liked Donald. He was full of fun, he didn't push or snatch, and he was just as ready to pass cakes at tea-time as to take them. The grown-ups liked him too, for he had good manners. As for Donald, he had never been so happy in his entire life.

But the loveliest thing of all was when the prizes were given! Who do you think won the first prize for the best fancy dress costume? Yes, Donald!

"But I can't take it," he said, "I wasn't asked to this party, really. That lady over there pulled me in. I'm only the little boy from next door, and this is the first party I've ever been to!"

"Well, of all the funny things!" cried the grown-ups. "We wondered who you were! But never mind, little boy – you deserve the first prize, so here it is – a clockwork railway train! And we hope you'll often come here and play with these children again."

Donald ran straight home with the first prize, and his mother was astonished!

"I shan't be lonely any more!" said Donald. And you may be sure he wasn't.

The
Remarkable
Tail

ONE day the toad who lived under the old mossy stone crawled out to have a drink from the water nearby. He was a wise old fellow, and nobody knew how long he had lived under his stone. No one dared to take the hole he lived in, for it belonged to the toad.

As the toad slid into the water, a perky little creature swam up to him.

"Hello, Toad! How are you?"

"Good morning," said the toad, swimming away. "And good-bye!"

"Ho! You think yourself very high and mighty, don't you?" said

the long-tailed creature,
swimming along by the toad.
"I've heard all about you – but I
don't think you are very
wonderful!"

The toad turned to look at this
cheeky creature. It was a newt in
his spring dress. He had a fine
wavy crest all down his back, and
a long, graceful tail. Underneath
he shone brightly with a
beautiful orange colour.

"Go away," said the toad.

"But I want to talk like you,"
said the newt. "Why does
everyone think you are so wise?
You don't look it! I think you are
an ugly creature! You have no

graceful tail as I have! And look at my beautiful orange tummy!"

"I don't want to," said the toad. It looks like one of those horrid-smelling toadstools that grow in the woods in autumn."

"I do think you look odd without a tail!" said the cheeky newt. "Why don't you try and grow one?"

"Why should I?" said the toad. "I am a wise toad, not a foolish newt like you!"

With that he turned and swam to the edge of the pond. He crawled out and went back to his stone, thinking angrily of the newt. "He will come to a bad end!" thought the old toad. "Foolish young creature!"

The newt was very proud of having talked to the toad. He told everyone about it. "I showed him my tail, and my lovely orange colouring," he said. "And I waved my crest at him and told him he was an ugly fellow! He swam back to the bank feeling very sorry for himself, I can tell you! Oh, I am a grand fellow, I am! When I'm as old as that toad I shall be twice as wise as he is!"

The newt often used to leave the pond and go to the stone where the toad lived. This annoyed the toad, who liked to be alone. Besides, the newt liked flies for dinner, and was delighted to feast on caterpillar – and the toad liked these things very much too.

"Go away!" he said to the newt. "You are a cheeky youngster, and will come to a bad end. You are foolish to leave the pond like this, and come wandering up here. I am safe under my stone. You have no shelter and can easily be seen!"

"Fiddlesticks!" said the newt. "I am no coward like you! Who will catch me, I should like to know! I am on the look-out for any rat, or snake, or stoat!"

Sure enough, when the quiet rat came running up behind the newt, the little creature heard him, and at once slid through the grass to the water. Plop! He was in the pond at once!

Another time the grass-snake glided up and the newt shot off just in time. The toad heard the splash as he leapt into the pond. The snake wondered whether to swim after him or not, but decided to look under the stone and see if anyone was hiding there. But when he saw the old toad he drew back his head hurriedly. He had once struck at

a toad and tried to swallow him –
and the creature had covered
himself with such an evil-tasting
liquid that the snake had spat
him out in disgust. No! Toads
were not good to eat.

"Didn't I tell you that I could
always escape my enemies?" said
the newt, running up to the
toad's stone again, as soon as the
snake had gone. "You are slow,
Toad, but I am quick. You can
only crawl – but I can run. Don't
you think my tail looks extra well
today? The crest goes all the way
down to the end. I have been
told that I am the prettiest
creature in the pond."

"Well, you are certainly the most talkative," said the toad. "I am tired of you. For the twentieth time, Newt, go away, and find someone who likes listening to you. I do NOT!"

"I shall stay here," said the newt. "It is nice and comfortable here, and the sun is warm."

The toad said nothing more. He sat at the entrance to his hole and blinked. Then he saw something that made him stare upwards. A great bird was flying down to the pond. What a big bird it was! It flapped its huge wings so slowly, and trailed its long legs behind it.

"A heron!" thought the toad. "Ha! He is going to fish in the pond for frogs, newts or fish! He will see this silly newt – and that will be the end of him!"

But the toad was kind-hearted, and he called to the curled-up newt: "Go back to the pond! The heron is coming!"

"I don't believe you!" said the newt. "You are only saying that to get rid of me!"

The heron flew lower – and the newt suddenly saw the shadow of the great wings above him. In terror he tried to run away – but the heron landed beside him, thrust downwards with his strong beak, and stabbed at his tail. Then he picked up the newt by the tail, and was about to swallow him, when the toad called out loudly: "Break off your tail! Break off your tail!"

The frightened newt wriggled and snapped his long, graceful tail right off. He left it in the heron's mouth and fell down into the water. He used his little feet to swim along, and disappeared into a hole in the bank, tailless, scared – but safe!

The heron said "Kronk!" in a deep voice, and flew off. The newt's tail was not much of a dinner – but the heron knew of

another pond that was swarming
with frogs!

The toad crept out from his
stone and went to the pond. He
slipped into it and swam about
until he found the hole in which
the newt was hidden.

"Are you safe?" he croaked.

"Yes – but I have lost my beautiful tail," said the newt sadly. "Still, I am grateful to you for telling me of that trick."

"I saw a lizard play that trick on a rat once," said the toad. "Your tail will grow again."

He swam off and went back to his hole.

"That newt needed a lesson," he said to himself. "Now he has got it. Perhaps he will be a wiser newt in future."

The toad saw no more of the newt for many months – and then one day he saw him again outside his stone.

"Good-day, Toad," said the newt, in a humble voice. "I have not come to worry you – only to say that my tail has grown again, though it is not nearly so nice as it was before – and I am wiser now, and no longer think I am the most wonderful creature in the pond."

The toad crept out from under his stone and looked at the newt. Certainly his tail had grown – but what a stumpy one compared to his other!

"You may not be so beautiful now, but you are certainly nicer," said the toad. "Come and see me as often as you like. I think that we will be friends now!"

And now you may often see the newt talking to the toad by his stone. You will know him by his stumpy tail. Wasn't it lucky for him that the toad taught him the trick of breaking off his tail? No wonder he is grateful!

The
Most Peculiar
Knocker

IN Hurry-Up Village there lived some naughty goblin children called Tuffy, Smick and Woff. The tricks they got up to!

They would lean over the walls of people's back gardens and snip their clothes lines so that the clothes would tumble right down into the mud.

They would all climb up to the little bedroom that Tuffy had at the top of his house, and pour water down on passers-by. And then they would go up to people's front doors and knock loudly and run away.

So you can see that they were really a perfect nuisance. "There go Tuffy, Smick and Woff," the people would say, seeing the three children going down the street. "I wonder what mischief they're up to now?"

One day Mr Candleshoe came to live in the cottage at the end of the street. He was a funny old fellow, who always sang little songs to himself whenever he went out. Tuffy and the others thought it would be fine fun to tease him.

"He's got a wonderful new knocker on his door," said Tuffy. "It's a really strange one – just like a man's hand! I guess it must have been a magic one some time or other."

It certainly was a peculiar knocker. It knocked extremely loudly, too, but that was a good thing because Mr Candleshoe was rather deaf, and he wouldn't have heard if anyone had knocked softly.

"Ratta-tatta-TAT!" said the knocker, loudly, when the postman called.

"RATTA-TATTA-TAT!" it said, even more loudly, when Mr Candleshoe's friend Mr Sharp-Eye, called. Mr Sharp-Eye was a wizard, it was said. He knew a lot of spells, and Tuffy, Woff and Smick kept out of his way. They didn't like the way he looked at them when they met him!

"I feel he might turn me into a black beetle or something," said Smick, "and I don't like it."

Now, Tuffy soon found that it was fun to bang on Mr Candleshoe's knocker. The first time he did it, he had to deliver a parcel there. He crashed the knocker up and down.

"RATTA-TATTA-RATTA-TATTA!" The noise almost made Mr Candleshoe jump out of his skin.

"Jumping pigs and piglets!" he cried. "What's that?"

He hurried to the door, falling

over the mat on the way. Tuffy
thought it really was one of the
funniest things he had ever seen.

"Now don't you crash at my
door like that again," said Mr
Candleshoe, when he saw Tuffy.
"I won't have it! You're a bad
goblin. I shan't give you any
money for bringing the parcel."

"Ho!" thought Tuffy, going
down the steps. "Oho! So he
won't give me any money, the
mean old miser! Well I'll soon
make him wish he had!"

He went to find Smick and
Woff. He told them how he had
crashed on the knocker at Mr
Candleshoe's and made the old

man jump. "He's a mean fellow," said Tuffy. "We'll go and do a lot more crashing, shall we?"

So Smick used to go and knock loudly on his way to school in the morning, and Woff used to do it whenever he passed, which was quite often.

"Ratta-tatta-TAT! RATTA-TAT!" You should have heard that knocker going – morning, afternoon and evening! Mr Candleshoe would jump out of his chair and tear to the door – and nobody would be there!

He was puzzled at first. He thought whoever was there must be invisible. But they weren't, of course. They had just run away.

Then Mr Candleshoe gave up
coming to the door to open it.
But the very times he didn't go, it
would be the postman with a
parcel, or Mrs Lucy coming
along with a dish of hot cakes, or
the milkman asking if he wanted
any cream left that day.

"What am I to do, what am I to
do?" said poor old Candleshoe
to his friend, Mr Sharp-Eye.
"That knocker makes me jump
from morning to night – and
when I answer the door, there's
nobody there – and if I don't
answer it there's sure to be
somebody!"

"You want a little magic rubbed into the knocker!" said Sharp-Eye, with a grin. "That's what you want, my good friend. I'll put some there for you. Let's see – your knocker is in the shape of a big hand, isn't it? I'll just go and rub a little of my yellow ointment into it. You'll soon find out who comes and bangs on it, Mr Candleshoe. And your knocker will hold him tight for you!"

Mr Sharp-Eye rubbed in the magic ointment. Then he said goodbye to Mr Candleshoe and went home.

It wasn't long before Tuffy was

along that way again. He looked
up the street and down. Nobody
about. Now for a good old crash
on that knocker! He'd make Mr
Candleshoe fall out of his chair
with fright!

But it so happened that
Candleshoe had gone out just
after his friend had walked home
and there was nobody in his
cottage! So when Tuffy rapped
on the knocker, "RATTA-
TATTA-TAT," there was no one
indoors to hear it.

Tuffy had tight hold of the
knocker as he knocked – but
something strange happened
before he had finished. The brass

knocker, which was shaped like a hand, suddenly took hold of him! Yes, it twisted round, and held Tuffy's hand so tightly that he squealed!

"Oooh! What's happening? Ooh! Let go, let go! Ooooh!"

Tuffy couldn't take his hand away! The knocker had got it far too tightly. He pulled and he tugged, but it wasn't a bit of good, he couldn't get away.

Then he guessed what had happened. Mr Candleshoe had some magic in his knocker, and the knocker was busy using it! It would hold Tuffy there till Mr Candleshoe came back – and then what would happen?

Tuffy began to squeal. His two friends Smick and Woff came by and they stopped when they heard Tuffy's yells. "What's the matter?" they shouted in surprise.

"Come and pull, come and pull!" cried Tuffy. "This knocker's got hold of me!"

So Smick and Woff went to pull and, dear me, they pulled so hard that the knocker came right off the door! Then Tuffy raced home as fast as he could, afraid that Mr Candleshoe might come back and catch him if he stayed a moment longer.

The knocker still had hold of his hand! Tuffy couldn't get rid of it. It held tightly on to his fingers, and it wouldn't let them go at all!

Tuffy put it into ice-cold water. No good. He put it into very hot water and almost scalded the skin off his own hand. No good at all! The knocker held him as tightly as ever.

Then Tuffy knew that nothing would ever make the magic knocker let go of his hand, unless Candleshoe helped, and he began to howl.

In came his father and mother, alarmed. When they saw Tuffy and the knocker, they were even more astonished.

"Get it off, oh please get it off!" wept Tuffy.

"It's a knocker!" said his father. "And it looks like Candleshoe's, too. Tuffy, how did you come to get it like this?"

Tuffy wailed out his story. His father listened sternly. "Ah – at last you have found someone who can punish you for playing your silly, annoying tricks!" he said. "Well, Tuffy, either you will have to live with that knocker, or you will have to go to Mr Candleshoe and confess to him what has happened!"

"I'm afraid to do that, I'm

afraid!" howled Tuffy.

But he had to go in the end, because, you see, he couldn't write, or wash his hand properly, or even undress, with the knocker holding him by the hand like that!

"Ha!" said Candleshoe, when Tuffy stood before him, his face red with crying. "So it was you trying to be funny, bringing me to the door a dozen times a day! Well, I think that you've got a fine punishment!"

"Please take the knocker off my hand!" wept Tuffy. "Please take it off."

"I've got a new knocker now,"

said Mr Candleshoe. "I don't need that one. You can have it."

"I don't WANNNNNNT it!" wailed Tuffy. "Oh, take it off, Mr Candleshoe, and I'll never never be bad again."

"Well – I'll take it off," said Mr Candleshoe, "but I don't want it back. It can live with you, Tuffy. But I warn you – if you get up to any tricks, the knocker will chase you and try to take hold of your hand once more!"

And goodness me, it does! His father never needs to punish Tuffy now. Whenever he's naughty, the knocker jumps up from its corner, and chases him around the room. What a fine time that knocker has and no mistake! I'm sure Tuffy's sorry now that he ever played the silly game of knocking at doors and running away.

Little Rubbalong Plays a Trick

ONE day little Rubbalong was mending shoes in his mother's cottage, humming a little song.

"Tippety-tap,
My work I begin,
Tippety-tap,
And a nail goes in!
I use good leather
From heel to toe,
No matter the weather
Warm and dry will you go!"

He finished a shoe and threw it on one side. Then he picked up a pair of stout laced boots.

"Ma!" he called, "here's a pair

of Old Man Borrow's boots. He owes us for the last ones I did – and he borrowed some money from you, didn't he? Shall I mend this pair?"

Ma Rubbalong came over to look at them. She gave a little smile that meant mischief.

"Now you listen to me, Rubbalong," she said. "Old Man Borrow ought to have a lesson about borrowing and never paying back. I think we'll give it to him!"

"How, Ma?" asked Rubbalong, beginning to mend the boots.

"Well, Old Man Borrow is vain," said Ma. "We will give him

that pair of yellow leather laces for his boots. He'll be so proud of them. But I'll rub a Go-Tight spell on them."

"How will that work?" asked Rubbalong, beginning to smile.

"Whenever he meets anyone that he owes money to, or has borrowed things from without returning them, those laces will pull themselves so tight he'll hardly be able to walk!" said Ma. "And what is more, Rubbalong, we'll tell everyone about the spell! Old Man Borrow will be very surprised when he finds himself meeting so many people he owes money to!"

Rubbalong laughed. "What a joke! You're an absolute wonder at fitting the right spell to the right people, Ma!"

He mended the boots. Then he took the lovely yellow laces that Ma Rubbalong had rubbed with her Go-Tight spell, and he threaded them deftly through the holes. "There! And now here comes Old Man Borrow for his boots!" said Rubbalong. "I wonder if he'll pay me."

He didn't, of course. "I'll look in tomorrow with the money," he said. "I'm in a bit of a hurry today." And off he went with the boots under his arm

Well, little Rubbalong soon spread the news about that there was a spell on Old Man Borrow's boots. "If you see him wearing yellow laces go and meet him," said Rubbalong. "They'll pull themselves so tight that he'll hardly be able to walk! He won't pay you what he owes you then – but maybe those laces will make him pay up in the end!"

Well, all kinds of people set out to meet Old Man Borrow the first day he wore his mended boots, very proud indeed of the yellow laces in them. Mr Tuck-In was the first. He had lent Old Man Borrow five pounds and wanted it back. Old Man Borrow tried to slip down a side turning but Mr Tuck-In marched right up to him.

And those yellow laces pulled themselves tight. Tighter still. And then so tight that they almost cut into Old Man Borrow's legs. He looked down in fright.

He could hardly walk. He had to hobble beside Mr Tuck-In for quite a long way, promising to pay back the five pounds as soon as he could. He couldn't even run away!

The laces loosened as soon as Mr Tuck-In went. Old Man

Borrow heaved a sigh of relief.
How strange! What had
happened? Had his legs swollen
up suddenly and got too large for
his boots? He bent down and
loosened the laces a little.

Then he met Dame Scarey. She
hurried towards him to ask him
to return the ladder she had lent
him. And goodness gracious,
those laces tightened themselves
again, and Old Man Borrow
groaned in fright. He began to
hobble, and Dame Scarey smiled
to herself as she saw Ma
Rubbalong's spell working. She
spoke to him sternly about her
ladder and then left him. The

laces became loose again. Old Man Borrow just couldn't understand it!

The people he met that morning! And dear me, every one of them had lent Old Man Borrow something and spoke about it crossly. He began to feel most annoyed.

"There must be something wrong with these boots," he said at last. "I'll go and complain to little Rubbalong."

So off he went and complained loudly and bitterly. "It's not the boots," said Rubbalong. "It's the laces. There must be some spell on them. You'd better give me them back."

"Oh no," said Old Man Borrow, hastily. "I like them. Besides, you gave me them for nothing. They're very fine."

"All right. Keep them then," said little Rubbalong. "But let's find out if they have a spell on them or not. You say your boots felt very tight when you met Mr Tuck-In – you owe him five pounds, don't you? And Dame Scarey? You've still got her ladder, haven't you? And Mrs Well-I-Never – and Old Father Whiskers, and...well, dear me, how strange, Old Man Borrow! You owe something to all of these people!"

"What difference does that make to my boots?" said Old Man Borrow, sulkily.

"Well, let's just see," said Rubbalong. "Do your boots feel tight now? Oh, they do – you say the laces are cutting into your legs. Well, you owe me money, Old Man Borrow. Pay up, and see if the boots feel alright again. If they do, we'll know it has to be those laces!"

Old Man Borrow scowled, but he paid up.

And hey presto the laces loosened, and the boots no longer felt tight!

"There you are," said Rubbalong. "Just what I told you. Better give me those laces back, Old Man Borrow."

But the mean old fellow wasn't going to give back something he had got for nothing. He scowled again and went off. He'd just have to put up with the spell, if that was what it was!

He couldn't stand it for long, though – the laces could make themselves tighter still, and they did. And now Mr Tuck-In has got back his five pounds, and Dame Scarey has got her ladder, and everyone else is getting their things back too.

Ma Rubbalong did laugh. "Let's hope the spell will last a nice long time," she said. "By that time we will all be calling Old Man Borrow by a quite different name."

"Yes. Old Man Pay-Back!" said little Rubbalong. "And it will all be because of your yellow laces, Ma!"

Whats Happened to the Clock?

PATSY and William were busy putting out their railway on the playroom floor. It took a long time because there were so many rails to fit together, and some of them were rather difficult.

"After we've put all the rails out, we'll put up the signals, and the station, and the tunnel," said Patsy. "Isn't it a beautiful railway set, William?"

It certainly was. It had belonged to their Uncle Ronnie, and he had gone abroad and had given them the set he had had when he was a boy. He had looked after it carefully and everything was as good as new.

At last all the rails were fitted together, the station was put up, with little porters and passengers standing on the platform, and the tunnel was placed over one part of the line.

"Now for the signals, and then we can put the engine on the lines with the carriages and set it going," said William.

Patsy looked at the clock to see what time it was. She gave a cry. "Oh, dear! Just look at the time. It's only five minutes to our bedtime – and we've just come to the very nicest part of all – getting the train going!"

William frowned. "This

bedtime business! We always seem to have to go to bed just when we're in the middle of something exciting. Yesterday we had to go before we finished the pictures we were painting."

"And the night before that I couldn't finish the story I was reading," said Patsy. "Bother the clock. It goes much too fast."

"What's Mother doing?" said William suddenly.

"She's turning out the old chests on the landing," said Patsy, looking surprised, "Why?"

"Well – she won't guess how the time is going, then," said William, and he got up from the floor. He went to the clock and turned the hands so that instead of saying a quarter past seven, they said a quarter past six!

"There!" said William. "It's only a quarter past six. We've got another hour to play!"

"Oh, William!" said Patsy, shocked. "You can't do a thing like that."

"Well, I have," said William. "Mummy isn't wearing her watch today because the glass is broken and it's at the jeweller's. She'll come and look at this clock – and she'll think it's right – so then we'll have a whole hour extra to play in!"

Patsy didn't say any more. She wanted the extra hour. Perhaps Mother would never guess!

Mother called from the landing after a bit. "Surely it is getting near your bedtime, you two. What does the clock say?"

William looked at it. "Twenty five to seven," he called.

"Really? But surely it is later

than that?" said Mother. She popped her head in at the door and stared hard at the clock. "Dear me – how extraordinary. It does say twenty five to seven. Has it stopped?"

"No, it hasn't," said William not looking at his mother. He felt suddenly rather ashamed. Patsy did too. She turned very red in the face and her mother wondered why.

"Well – I suppose I must have mistaken the time," said Mother, and went to get on with her turning-out. The children didn't say anything to one another. They both wished they hadn't

put the clock back like that —
they had tricked Mother, and
that was a horrid thing to do.

"Do you think we ought to tell
Mother what we've done?"
asked Patsy, after a time.

"No," said William. "We've
done it and we might as well take
the extra hour."

So they didn't say a word to
Mother. They went to bed at
quarter past eight instead of
quarter past seven, feeling rather
tired – though the clock, of
course, only showed quarter
past seven!

Next morning the clock
appeared to be quite right again.

When the children heard the eight o'clock hooter going, far away in the town, the clock said eight o'clock too. How had it got itself right again? They looked at Mother, wondering if she would say anything about it, but she didn't say a word.

They went to school as usual, stayed there to dinner, and came back to tea. They did their homework and then went up to the playroom to go on playing with their railway. It looked very exciting indeed, all set out there.

"I'll have one engine and you have the other," said William. They were lucky because there were two engines, and it was fun to set them both going and switch them from one line to another just when it seemed as if there was going to be a collision.

They played for what seemed a very little while, when Mummy put in her head.

"Not much more time," she said. "Make the best of what time is left before going to bed."

The children were astonished. Why, surely it couldn't be more than six o'clock! They had hardly played any time at all! They glanced at the clock.

"Why – it says five past seven!" cried Patsy. "It can't be five past seven. It simply can't."

"No – it can't," said William. But certainly the clock said five past seven.

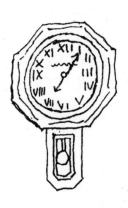

"Shall I alter it again?" said William.

"No – don't," said Patsy at once. "For one thing, Mother has seen the time – and for another I don't want to trick her again. I felt dreadful about that. I think we ought to have owned up when she came to kiss us goodnight – and we didn't."

They argued about the time for a while, then Mother called in from the bathroom. "What's the time by the clock, children? Surely it's bedtime now?"

They looked at the clock. It said a quarter past seven.

"Mother, the clock says a quarter past seven," called William. "But it can't be! What's happened to the clock? I'm sure it isn't right."

"Dear me – a quarter past

seven already," said Mother. "Well, you must certainly go to bed then. Just tidy up quickly and come along. You can leave your rails out, of course."

So the children had to leave their railway before they had set the engines going for more than once or twice round the rails. It was very disappointing.

They washed, brushed their teeth and hair, and got into bed. Mother said she would bring them some cocoa.

Whilst they were sitting up in bed, still feeling gloomy, William heard the church clock beginning to strike. He listened and counted.

"One-two-three-four-five-six-seven-why, it only struck seven times. It's seven o'clock, not eight o'clock."

"We've come to bed a whole hour early," said Patsy.

"Mother!" called William. "The church clock has just struck seven. It isn't eight o'clock. It's seven. We've missed a whole hour's play."

"The playroom clock says eight o'clock," said Mother. "You went by that yesterday, didn't you – so you must go by it today."

Mother sounded rather stern. Patsy looked at her and burst into tears. "Mother! We put the clock back yesterday so that we could have a whole hour's extra play. We were horrid!"

"Yes, it was rather horrid," said Mother. "I really thought it was just a trick and that you'd own up, you know, when I kissed you good night. Then I saw that you really did mean to deceive me. And now the clock has paid you back! It's an hour before its time instead of an hour after."

"Mother," said William, "I believe you've played a trick, haven't you? If you haven't, what's happened to the clock?"

"Of course I've played you a trick," said Mother laughing. "Exactly the same trick that you played me, but the other way round. Now drink your cocoa and go to sleep."

"Mother, I'm very sorry," said Patsy, rubbing her eyes. "I felt quite dreadful about it. I'm glad you played us a trick too – now we're quits!"

"Yes – we're quits!" said Mother, and she kissed her and

William, too. "You gained an hour and lost an hour and perhaps learnt a lesson – so we won't say any more about it."

They didn't – and you won't be surprised to hear that the playroom clock has behaved in quite an ordinary way ever since!

How the
Wild Roses
Grew Tall

OLD Dame Kirri was a witch.
You could tell she was
because she had bright green
eyes. She was a good witch
though, and spent most of her
time making good spells to help
people who were ill or unhappy.

She lived in Toppling Cottage,
which was just like its name, and
looked exactly as if it was going
to topple over. But it was kept up
by strong magic, and not a brick
had fallen although the cottage
was five hundred years old.

At the back of the cottage was
the witch's garden. Round it ran
a very, very high wall, taller than
the tallest man.

"I like a high wall. It keeps people from peeping and prying," said old Dame Kirri. "In my garden I grow a lot of strange and powerful herbs. I don't want people to see them and steal them. I won't have people making spells from my magic herbs – they might easily make bad ones."

The witch had a cat. He was black and big, and had green eyes very like the witch's own eyes. His name was Cinder-Boy.

Cinder-Boy helped the witch in her spells. He was really a remarkably clever cat. He knew how to sit exactly in the middle

of a chalk ring without moving,
whilst Kirri the witch danced
round and sang spells. He knew
how to go out and collect dew-
drops in the moonlight. He took
a special little silver cup for that
and never spilt a drop.

He never drank milk. He liked
tea, made as strong as the witch
made for herself. Sometimes he
would sit and sip his tea and purr,
and the witch would sip her tea
and purr too. It was funny to see
them.

Cinder-Boy loved to sleep in
the walled-in garden. He knew
all the flowers and herbs there.
No weed was allowed to grow,

though, because Cinder-Boy
scratched them all up.

But one day he came to a small
plant growing at the foot of the
wall. It had leaves like a rose-
tree. It had pale pink flowers,
with a mass of yellow stamens in
the middle. It smelled very
sweet.

"What flower are you?" asked
Cinder-Boy. "You smell rather
like a rose."

"Well, that's just what I am,"
said the plant. "I'm a wild rose."

"How did you get in here?"
asked Cinder-Boy, surprised.

"A bird dropped a seed," said
the wild rose. "But I don't like

being here, black cat."

"My name is Cinder-Boy," said the witch's cat. "Why don't you like being here? It's a very nice place to be."

"Well, I feel shut in," said the wild rose. "I'm not very large. If I was taller I could see over the top of the wall. I don't like being right down here at the bottom, all shut in."

"Well, grow tall then," said Cinder-Boy. "I can give you a spell to make your stems nice and long if you like. Then you can reach up to the top of the wall and look over. There's a nice view there, I can tell you."

"Oh, would you do that?" said the wild rose in delight. "That would be lovely. Thank you!"

So Cinder-Boy went off to get a spell to make the stems of the wild rose grow very long. He soon found one. It was in a small blue bottle, and he poured it into a watering-can. The spell was blue, too.

Then he watered the wild rose with the spell, and it began to work almost at once. In two or three days the stems of the wild rose plant had grown quite high into the air.

"Go on growing. You will soon find that you have got to the top of the wall!" said Cinder-Boy.

So the wild rose went on making its stems longer and longer, hoping to get to the very top of the wall.

But when Cinder-Boy strolled out into the garden to see how it was getting on, what a shock he had! Every single stem was bent over and they all lay sprawling on the grass!

"Why, what has happened?" said Cinder-Boy, waving his tail in surprise.

"My stalks grew tall, but they didn't grow strong," said the wild rose sadly. "Just as I reached the top of the wall, they all flopped over and fell down. They are not strong enough to bear their own weight."

"Well, how do plants with weak stems manage to climb high then?" asked Cinder-Boy, puzzled. "Runner beans grow high and they have very weak stems. Sweet peas grow high, and they have weak stems too. I'll go and see how they do it."

So off he went, for the witch grew both in her back garden. He soon came back.

"The beans twine their stalks around poles," he said, "and the sweet peas grow little green fingers, called tendrils, which catch hold of things, and they pull themselves up high like that. Can't you do that?"

The wild rose couldn't. It didn't know how. Its stems wouldn't twist themselves, however much it tried to make them do so. And it couldn't grow a tendril at all.

"Well, we must think of another way," said the cat.

"Cinder-Boy, how do you get up to the top of the wall?" asked the wild rose. "You are often up there in the sun. I see you. Well, how do you get to the top?"

"I run up the trees," said Cinder-Boy. "Do you see the young fruit trees near you? Well,

I run up those to the top of the wall. I use my claws to help me. I dig them into the bark of the trees, and hold on with them."

He showed the wild rose his big, curved claws. "I can put them in or out as I like," he said. "They are very useful claws."

The wild rose thought they were too. "If I grew claws like that I could easily climb up the fruit trees, right through them to the top, and then I'd be waving at the top of the wall," it said. "Can't you get me some claws like yours, Cinder-Boy?"

The cat blinked his green eyes and thought hard. "I know what

I could do," he said. "I could ask the witch Kirri, my mistress, to make some magic claws that would grow on you. I'll ask her today. In return you must promise to grow her some lovely scarlet hip berries that she can trim her hats and bonnets with in the autumn."

"Oh, I will, I will," promised the wild rose.

So Cinder-Boy went off to the witch Kirri, and told her what he wanted.

She grumbled a little. "It is difficult to make claws," she said. "Very difficult. You will have to help me, Cinder-Boy. You will have to sit in the middle of a blue ring of chalk, and put out all your claws at once, whilst I sing a magic song. Don't be scared at what happens."

Cinder-Boy went to sit in the middle of a chalk ring that the witch drew in the middle of the garden. He stuck out all his claws as she commanded.

She danced round with her broomstick, singing such a magic song that Cinder-Boy felt quite scared. Then a funny thing happened.

His claws fell out on to the ground with a clatter – and they turned red or green as they fell.

He looked at his claws and saw
new ones growing. Then those
fell out, too. How very, very
strange it all was!

Soon there was quite a pile of
claws on the ground. Then the
witch stopped singing and
dancing, and rubbed out the ring
of chalk.

"You can come out now,
Cinder-Boy," she said. "The
magic is finished."

Cinder-Boy collected all the
red and green claws. They were
strong and curved and sharp. He
took them to the bottom of the
garden to the wild rose.

"I've got claws for you!" he

said. "The witch Kirri did some strong magic. Look, here they are. I'll press each one into your stems, till you have claws all down them. Then I'll say a growing spell, and they will grow into you properly, and then they will belong to you.

So Cinder-Boy did that, and soon the wild rose felt the cat-claws growing firmly into its long stems.

"Now," said Cinder-Boy, in excitement, "now you will be able to climb right up through the fruit tree, wild rose. I will help you at first."

So Cinder-Boy took the wild

rose stems, all set with claws, and pushed them up into the little fruit tree that grew near by. The claws took hold of the bark and held on firmly. Soon all the stems were climbing up high through the little fruit tree, the claws digging themselves into the trunk and branches.

The wild rose grew higher. It pulled itself up by its new claws. It was at the top of the wall! It could see right over it to the big world beyond.

"Now I'm happy!" said the wild rose to Cinder-Boy. "Come and sit up here on the wall beside me. Let us look at the big world together. Oh, Cinder-Boy, it is lovely up here. I am not shut in any longer. Thank you for my claws. I do hope I shall go on growing them now."

It did. And it grew beautiful scarlet berries in the autumn for witch Kirri's winter bonnets. You should see how pretty they are when she trims them with the rose hips!

Ever since that day the wild roses have grown cat's claws all down their stems, sometimes green and sometimes red or pink. They use them for climbing. Have you seen them? If you haven't, do go and look.

Plum Jam

"I wish I had some plums to make plum jam," said Lightfoot the pixie to Prickles. Prickles the hedgehog was her neighbour. He lived under the hedge where Lightfoot had her tiny house.

"Buy some," said Prickles.

"I haven't any money," said Lightfoot. She never had! She left her purse about everywhere, and the little red imps were always running off with it.

"Well – go and ask Mr Frowny for some," said Prickles. "Go on! Take your basket with you. He's got a lot of plum trees, and there are quite a lot of plums on the ground. He doesn't even bother to pick them up!"

"Oh, I daren't ask him," said Lightfoot. "He's always so cross, and he's got such dreadful eyebrows to frown with. I wouldn't ask him for anything. You go, Pickles. Can't you go for me? If you will, I'll give you a pot of my plum jam all for yourself. You can spread it on the toadstools you like to eat so much and make a meal of toadstool and jam. Lovely!"

"It does sound nice," said Prickles. "Well, I'm not afraid of Mr Frowny. He can waggle his big eyebrows at me all he likes, and I shan't mind a bit!"

"All right, then – you go along," said Lightfoot. And Prickles ran off, his little bright eyes looking round and about for slugs as he went. He liked a meal of slugs. He thought they were even nicer than beetles.

He came to Mr Frowny's house. Mr Frowny was in his garden, weeding. Prickles ran up to him. "Please, Mr Frowny, may I have some of your plums?"

"What! Do you think you can climb trees and pick plums?" said Mr Frowny.

"Oh, no. But I could take some of these that are on the ground," said Prickles.

"And how many could you take in that little mouth of yours?" said Mr Frowny. "You need your legs to run with, so you can't carry any with those. Ho,ho! You could only take half a plum, Pickles!"

"Well, may I go and take some, Mr Frowny?" asked Pickles. "Please say yes. I'll do you a good turn, if you like, in payment."

"And pray what good turn can you do me?" asked Mr Frowny, waggling his enormous eyebrows to scare Prickles.

But Prickles wasn't a bit

scared. "Please, sir, I will come and gobble up all your slugs," he said. "They feast on your lettuces, don't they? Well, I'll save your lettuces if I eat up all your slugs!"

"Very well," said Mr Frowny. "You can go and take as many plums as you can carry – but you'll only be able to carry half a plum in that silly mouth of yours. Ho, ho, ho!"

Prickles ran off. He went into the orchard, and he looked for a plum tree. Ah, there was one, a nice early tree, thick with little round red plums. Lovely!

Prickles ran to the tree. There

were such a lot on the ground.
Did he pick them up in his small
mouth, or try to carry some off in
his front paws?

No, he had a much better idea
than that! What do you think he
did? He curled himself tightly
into a ball of prickles, and then
he rolled himself round and
round and round under the plum
tree, all among the fallen plums.

What happened? Why, a great
many plums stuck to his prickles!
When he uncurled himself at last
there were the plums, sticking all
over him.

He ran out of the gate, and Mr
Frowny saw him. He stared in

surprise. "Hey! What's the matter with you? You do look queer! My goodness me – you're stuck all over with plums! So that's how you're going to take them away! Come back!"

But Prickles didn't come back. He scuttled down the lane, into the field, and ran down the hedge till he came to where Lightfoot was sewing outside her little house. She jumped up with a squeal.

"Oh! Whatever's this! Gracious – it's you, Prickles – but what have you done to yourself?"

"Brought you some plums to make plum jam, of course," said

Prickles proudly. "Aren't I clever? Now you just take them all off my prickles one by one, Lightfoot, and wash them. Then get out your sugar, ready to make jam. You will be able to make a nice lot!"

"You clever little thing!" cried Lightfoot. "I'd kiss you if there were anywhere to kiss!"

"There's my nose," said Prickles. "But I don't much like being kissed. I'd rather have a pot of jam."

"You shall have one!" said Lightfoot, pleased. "I'll make you some straight away, and we'll have it for tea. You must come to tea with me today."

She set to work to make the jam. Soon it was bubbling on the little stove, smelling very good indeed. Prickles sniffed hard. It would be very nice to spread on toadstools!

He went to tea with Lightfoot that afternoon. Outside her tiny house grew a little ring of toadstools. Prickles spread some plum jam on the top of one, and then nibbled it all round the edge till it was gone.

"Delicious!" he said. "Best I ever tasted. Thank you very much, Lightfoot."

"Now you take this pot away

with you, and you can spread plum jam on your toadstools every day," said Lightfoot. "You deserve it for your cleverness!"

Prickles kept his word to Mr Frowny. He ate all his slugs for him, and now Mr Frowny has the finest lettuces in the town. So, you see, everybody was pleased!

Betty's
Fairy Doll

IT all began on a day when Betty was walking with her doll's pram by the Big Pond at the end of the lane. She was going along by herself, thinking of the delicious ginger buns that Mother had promised to make her for tea – and suddenly she heard a splash, and saw some big ripples on the pond.

"Something's fallen in!" she thought to herself, and she stopped in surprise and looked. At first she couldn't see anything at all in the pond, but then she saw a tiny little black thing which was bobbing about a good way out in the middle.

Whatever could it be?

Then Betty heard a little high voice: "Help! Help!"

"Gracious, whatever is it?" wondered Betty in alarm. She quickly broke a long twig off a nearby bush and tried to reach out to the little black bobbing thing with it — and to her enormous surprise the thing clung on to it at once!

"Pull me in, pull me in!" she heard it cry. So she pulled the twig and then found that holding tightly to the end of it was – whatever do you think! – a little dark-haired fairy, with wet, bedraggled wings, looking very frightened and cold.

"Oh, thank you, thank you so very much!" said the little creature. "You saved my life! I was talking to Bushy the Squirrel up in the tree there and I seem to have lost my balance and fallen into the water."

"How are you going to get dry?" asked Betty, gazing in surprise at the wet fairy. "You do look so wet and cold."

"I don't know," said the fairy. "But perhaps I can fly off somewhere and dry myself with a dead leaf."

She tried to spread her dripping wings – and then she

gave a cry of dismay.

"Oh! My wings are hurt! They are all bent! I shall have to grow new ones now before I will be able to fly again. Whatever shall I do?"

Then Betty had a splendid idea. She clapped her hands at the thought of it.

"Oh, do come home with me!" she begged. "I have a dear little dolls' house with a nice bed in it where you can sleep. I have lots of doll's clothes that would fit you perfectly, and there's a lovely dolls' bath you can wash in. You could live with me till your wings had grown again.

Do say you will! It would be so lovely for me, because I haven't any brothers or sisters, and I'd love to have a fairy to play with."

"It really is very kind of you," said the fairy, shivering. "Are you sure I shan't be in the way? You won't tell anybody about me, will you?"

"Of course I won't!" said Betty. "It shall be a real secret. I'm very good at keeping secrets, you know. And you won't be in the way at all – I'd simply love to have you."

"A-tishoo, a-tishoo!" sneezed the fairy, suddenly.

"Oh dear, I think you must be

catching cold already!" cried
Betty. "Quick, wrap this doll's
shawl round you and I'll put you
in the pram and wheel you home
to my bedroom. There's a lovely
fire there."

The fairy wrapped the wooly
shawl round her and then Betty
lifted the little creature into the
pram. She hurried home, and
when at last she was safely in
her own bedroom she took out
the fairy and stood her in front of
the fire.

"Take off your wet clothes,"
she said to the fairy. "I'm going
to find some nice warm ones out
of my doll's wardrobe. I've some

that will just fit you."

The fairy slipped off her wet
clothes, and dried herself on a
little towel that Betty gave her.
Then she dressed herself in the
doll's clothes, which fitted her
really beautifully. The dress was
pale blue and the stockings and
shoes matched. The fairy thought
she looked very nice.

"What is your name?" asked
Betty. "Mine's Betty."

"Mine is Tippitty," said the
fairy. "I say, would you mind
terribly finding some scissors so
that you can clip off my wings
for me, please?"

"Clip off your wings!" said

Betty, in great surprise. "But whatever for?"

"Well, my new ones won't grow till the old ones are clipped off," said Tippitty. "It won't hurt me. Just take your scissors and cut them off, please."

So Betty took the scissors from her sewing box and clipped the fairy's wings off. It seemed such a pity, but still, if new ones would grow soon, perhaps it didn't matter. Betty put the clipped-off wings into a box to keep. They were so pretty – just like a butterfly's powdery wings.

"I'd better pretend to be one of your dolls if anyone comes in,"

said Tippitty, doing up her blue
shoes. "Listen! Is that someone
coming now?"

"Yes, it's Auntie Jane coming
to tell me it's time for tea," said
Betty. "Daddy is out today, so
we're having our tea early."

The door opened and Auntie
Jane came in.

"Your Mummy wants you to
come down to tea now," she said.
"Hurry up, because there are
ginger buns for you."

Betty looked at the fairy. She
had made herself stiff and
straight, just like a doll. Nobody
would know she was a fairy and
not a doll.

"Tell Mummy I'm just coming," said Betty. She washed her hands, brushed her hair, told the fairy to keep warm by the fire, and then went downstairs to have tea.

"Mummy, may I have some milk, some biscuits and a ginger bun?" asked Betty when she had finished her tea. "I want to play with my doll's tea-set."

"Yes, dear," said Mummy. "Take what you want. I will come up to you at bedtime. Play quietly till then."

Betty was pleased. She took the jug of milk, four biscuits and a bun. Then off she ran upstairs.

The fairy was still by the fire, looking much better, though she still kept sneezing.

Betty got out her tea-set and poured the milk into the tea-pot. She put the biscuits on a plate and the bun on another plate. Then she called the fairy to have her tea.

The cup was just the right size for her to drink from, and she was very pleased. She ate a good tea and then Betty said she had better go to bed in case her cold got worse.

The little girl undressed the fairy carefully. It was just like having a real live doll. She brushed the pretty dark hair, all curly, and then told the fairy she could wash in the doll's bath if she liked.

There was one bed in the doll's house which was much bigger than the rest. The fairy climbed into that and Betty covered her up and tucked her in.

"I'm so sleepy," said Tippitty, yawning. "I think I shall soon be asleep."

"I'll sing you to sleep," said Betty. So she sang all the nursery rhymes she knew in a soft little voice, and very soon the fairy was fast asleep. Betty shut the front of the dolls' house just as

Mummy came up to say it was bedtime. She longed to show Mummy the fairy in the doll's bed, but it was a secret and so she couldn't.

Tippitty lived with Betty for three weeks, until her new wings grew. At first she kept them neatly folded under her dress, but when they grew larger Betty cut a hole in the blue frock and the wings grew out of the hole. It was most exciting to watch them.

Betty took Tippitty out in her doll's pram each day for a walk. She gave her her meals out of the doll's cups and dishes. She played with her and told her stories. The fairy thought she had never ever met such a nice little girl in all her life.

At last the time came for Tippitty to go. Her new wings had quite grown and were beautiful. The fairy could fly well with them, and there was no need for her to stay with Betty any longer.

But she was very sorry to go – and as for Betty, she couldn't bear to think that she wouldn't have her small playmate any longer. She cried when the fairy said she must say good-bye.

"You have been so good and kind to me, Betty," said Tippitty.

"Is there anything I can do for you? Anything at all?"

"I suppose you couldn't give me a baby brother or sister, could you?" asked Betty. "It's so lonely being the only child. I haven't anyone to play with or love. I wish I could have a baby brother or sister!"

"I'll see what I can do for you," promised Tippitty. She kissed Betty, spread her wings, and flew to the window. "I'll come back and see you sometimes," she said, and off she went.

Betty was very lonely when she was gone. She often took out the box in which she had put the clipped-off wings, and looked at them, wishing and wishing that Tippitty would come back and live with her.

And then one morning a wonderful thing happened. Auntie Jane came to her room and woke her up, and said: "Betty, just fancy! You've got a little baby brother! He came in the night!"

Betty sprang up in bed in delight. So her wish had come true! Oh, how perfectly lovely! She wasn't going to be an only child any more – the fairy had granted her wish.

"Oh, I wish we could call the

baby Tippitty!" said Betty. "Do you think Mummy would agree, Auntie Jane?"

"Goodness me, whatever for?" asked Auntie Jane, in astonishment. "I never heard such a name before. What put it into your head, child?"

But Betty wouldn't tell her. The baby was called Robin, and Betty loved him very much – far more than she had loved Tippitty. Mummy soon let her hold him and carry him, and one evening she even let Betty bath him.

Tippitty happened to look in at the window just as Betty was bathing the baby – but Betty didn't even see her. She was far too happy. Tippitty smiled and flew away.

"Betty will never miss me now!" she said. "She's got somebody better!"